The Little Princess
Who Wouldn't Brush Her Hair

Written & Illustrated by Nicole Donoho

ISBN: 1481023713
ISBN-13: 978-1481023719

INSPIRED BY NANA JULIE'S LITTLE PRINCESS, KAITLYN,
WHO WOULDN'T BRUSH HER HAIR

Once there was a little princess.
She was a beautiful little princess.
And she wore a beautiful purple dress.

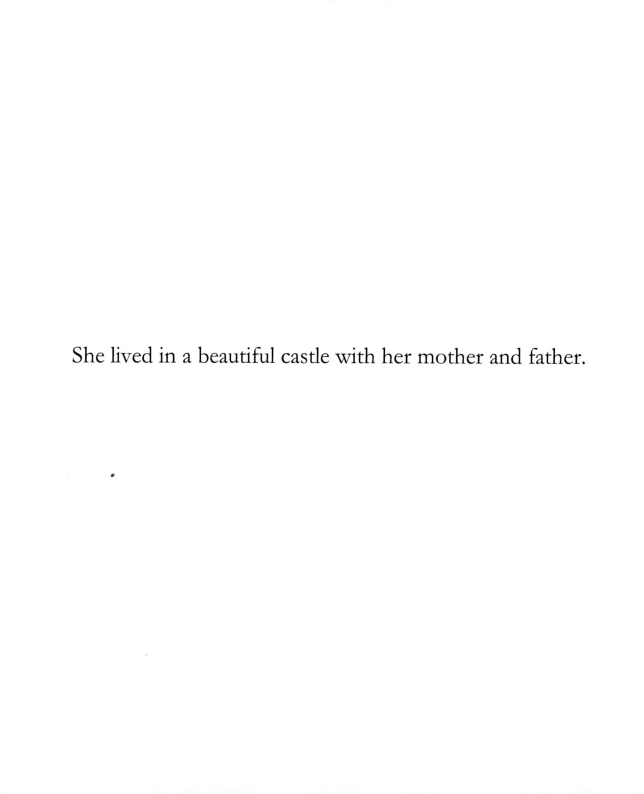

She lived in a beautiful castle with her mother and father.

She owned a beautiful little puppy.

And she had beautiful curly hair.

But the little princess did one thing that was not so beautiful. She would not brush her beautiful curly hair.

Her mother tried to brush the little princess's hair.

The little princess screamed. "No! It hurts."

And so her beautiful curly hair stayed tangled all the time.
Her curly hair became so tangled that one day…

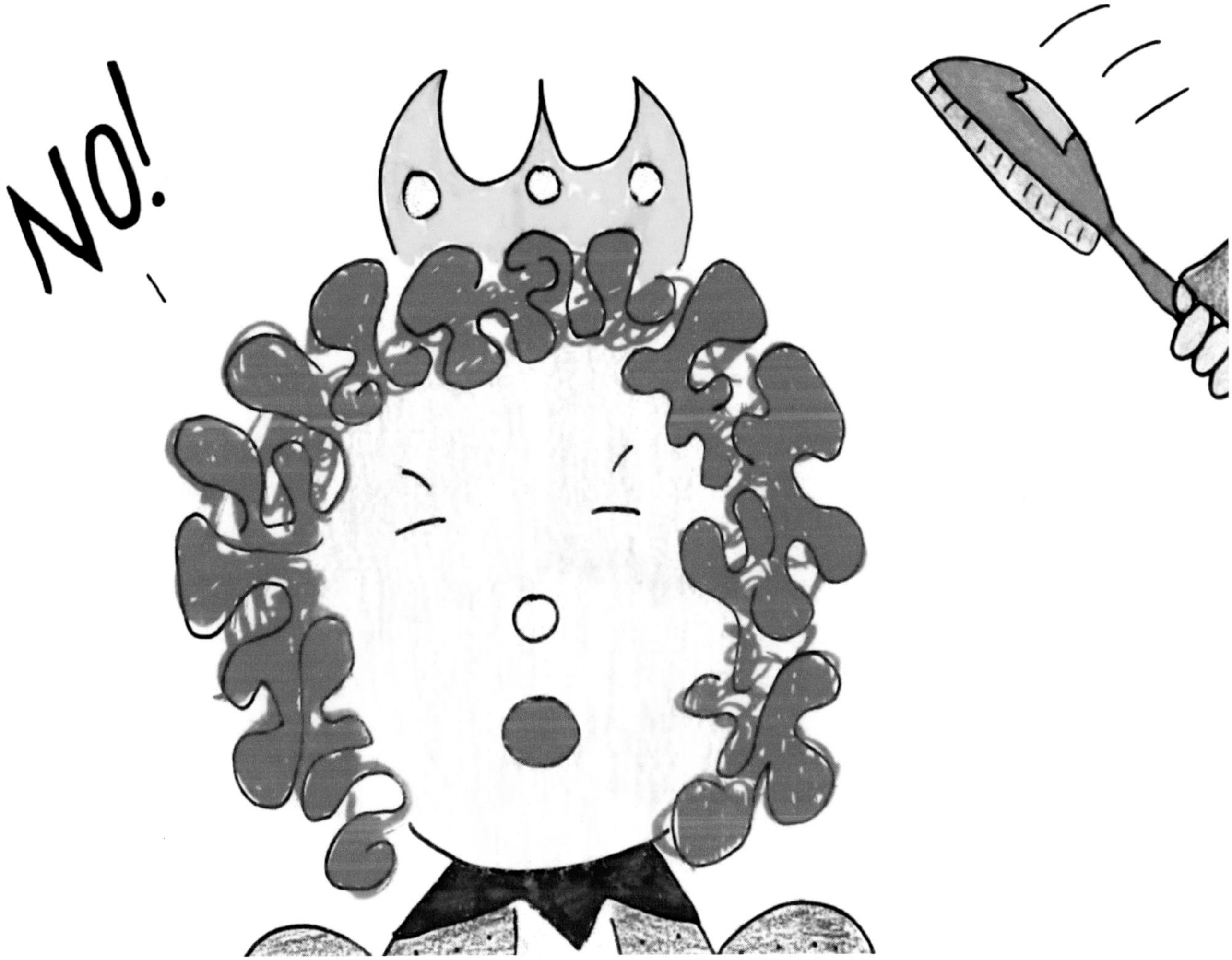
No!

...it swallowed her hairbrush.

"This is great!" the little princess smiled, "Now I won't have to brush my hair ever again."

The little princess sat down for dinner.
While she was eating her curly hair swallowed her crown.

"That's okay." The little princess smiled, "It wasn't shiny enough anyway."

The little princess went to sleep in her beautiful little bed.
The next morning when she woke up…

…her curly hair had swallowed her pillow.

"That's okay." The little princess smiled, "It wasn't soft enough anyway."

The little princess ran outside to play catch with her puppy.
She threw the ball and her curly hair reached out and swallowed it.

"That's okay." The little princess smiled, "It wasn't his favorite toy anyway."

"Oh, my little princess." Her mother cried,
"Please let me brush your beautiful hair before it gets worse."

"No!" the little princess screamed and ran outside to play on her swing.

The little princess loved to play on her swing.
She loved to swing really high.
But the little princess swung so high…

…that her curly hair got tangled in the tree limbs.
"Oh no!" the little princess cried, "Help!"

"Little princess, what have you done?" her mother cried.

She pulled on the little princess but her hair was stuck tight in the limbs of the tree.

Her father tried pulling the little princess out too
but she would not budge.

"Well, my little princess there is only one way to get you down."
Her father sighed, "I will have to cut your curly hair."

"Not my hair!" the little princess cried.

"It's the only way to get you down."
Her father said as he cut her beautiful curly hair.

The little princess looked in the mirror.
All her beautiful curly hair was gone.
The little princess was so sad.

As the little princess was crying a beautiful little fairy appeared.

"Hello, little princess, I am here to grant you a wish and make you happy again. But you can only have one wish."

The little princess smiled and told the fairy.
"I want my beautiful hair back."

"Oh no, you will have to make another wish." The fairy told the little princess, "I can't give beautiful hair to a little princess that won't brush it."

"Oh please, little fairy, if you give me back my hair I will brush it every day."
The little princess cried.

The fairy disappeared and the little princess fell back asleep.

The next morning the little princess ran to the mirror.
Her beautiful curly hair was back.
She ran downstairs to show her mother and father.

"Little princess, your beautiful hair is back." Her mother smiled, "We'll have to buy you a beautiful new crown to wear with it."

"No, Mother," the little princess said, "I don't want a new crown."

"What do you want, little princess?" her father asked.

"A beautiful new hairbrush!" the little princess smiled, "So I can brush my beautiful curly hair."

The End

For other books by Nicole Donoho visit:
www.facebook.com/nicoledonohobooks

35638247R00033

Made in the USA
Lexington, KY
06 April 2019